Dear Parents:

Congratulations! Your child is taking the first steps on an exciting journey. The destination? Independent reading!

STEP INTO READING® will help your child get there. The program offers five steps to reading success. Each step includes fun stories and colorful art or photographs. In addition to original fiction and books with favorite characters, there are Step into Reading Non-Fiction Readers, Phonics Readers and Boxed Sets, Sticker Readers, and Comic Readers—a complete literacy program with something to interest every child.

Learning to Read, Step by Step!

Ready to Read   Preschool–Kindergarten
• big type and easy words • rhyme and rhythm • picture clues
For children who know the alphabet and are eager to begin reading.

Reading with Help   Preschool–Grade 1
• basic vocabulary • short sentences • simple stories
For children who recognize familiar words and sound out new words with help.

Reading on Your Own   Grades 1–3
• engaging characters • easy-to-follow plots • popular topics
For children who are ready to read on their own.

Reading Paragraphs   Grades 2–3
• challenging vocabulary • short paragraphs • exciting stories
For newly independent readers who read simple sentences with confidence.

Ready for Chapters   Grades 2–4
• chapters • longer paragraphs • full-color art
For children who want to take the plunge into chapter books but still like colorful pictures.

STEP INTO READING® is designed to give every child a successful reading experience. The grade levels are only guides; children will progress through the steps at their own speed, developing confidence in their reading.

Remember, a lifetime love of reading starts with a single step!

© 2016 Universal Studios Licensing LLC. "The Secret Life of Pets" is a trademark and copyright of Universal Studios. Licensed by Universal Studios Licensing LLC. All rights reserved.

Published in the United States by Random House Children's Books, a division of Penguin Random House LLC, 1745 Broadway, New York, NY 10019, and in Canada by Penguin Random House Canada Limited, Toronto.

Step into Reading, Random House, and the Random House colophon are registered trademarks of Penguin Random House LLC.

Visit us on the Web!
StepIntoReading.com
randomhousekids.com

Educators and librarians, for a variety of teaching tools, visit us at
RHTeachersLibrarians.com

ISBN 978-0-399-55497-1 (trade) — ISBN 978-0-399-55498-8 (lib. bdg.) —
ISBN 978-0-399-55499-5 (ebook)

Printed in the United States of America

10 9 8 7 6 5 4 3 2 1

ILLUMINATION PRESENTS

THE SECRET LIFE OF

PeTs

DOG DAYS

by Andrea Posner-Sanchez

Random House 🏠 New York

WITHDRAWN

This is Max.

He lives in New York
with his owner, Katie.

Max and Katie
love each other.
Max is a lucky dog!

But every day,

Katie leaves.

Max's friends live in
his building.
They all hang out
when their owners
are not home.

Gidget is a fluffy dog.

She loves Max.

Chloe is a fat cat.

She loves to eat.

But she does not like

cat food.

This chicken looks good!
Yum!

Time for dessert!

Buddy likes back rubs.
When his owner is out,
a food mixer
does the job!

Mel does not like
squirrels.
He barks every time
one goes by his window.

Katie comes home
with a surprise.

Another dog will live
with her and Max!
His name is Duke.

Max and Duke

do not get along.

Duke tries to
get rid of Max.

They get caught
by a dogcatcher
and locked in a cage.

A bunny helps get
Max and Duke out.
But now they are lost.

Gidget is worried.
She flies around
on a hawk,
looking for Max.

Gidget gets
all the pets to help.
Where are Max
and Duke?

Max and Duke are
(in) a sausage factory.

The food is yummy,
but they want to
find their home.

Now Max and Duke
are friends.
When they get home
to Katie, they are
a happy family!